Dress Code:
The Organization

Expect the Unexpected

Dedicated to

the best english teacher I've ever met, Pernilla
and most importantly
everyone that has truly believed in me

© 2022 Decirée Baard
Förlag: BoD – Books on Demand, Stockholm, Sverige
Tryck: BoD – Books on Demand, Norderstedt, Tyskland
ISBN: 978-91-8027-967-3

Chapter One

Jasmin drags her hand over her face and realizes she had fallen asleep on the couch. She gets up and looks at her phone: 06.39, she still has time. She goes to the fridge and takes a look around, nothing that she likes.

The phone starts to ring, Jasmin answers and a voice says "five minutes." Jasmin lifts her purse off the ground and takes up a gun. A car door closes and a man walks up towards the house, she hears the keys in the door and the man goes inside. He takes off his shoes and goes to the living room, where Jasmin is standing and waiting.

"Hello, Charlie!"

"Who are you?" Charlie askes as Jasmin points her gun at him.

"I have money in my wallet here, take it."

"I'm very sorry you got dragged into this, you have a very beautiful family."

Her finger lets go of the trigger and the bullet hits Charlie in the chest. He's leaning towards a wall and Jasmin takes his hand and says "everything is gonna be alright, I'm here with you."

After a while Jasmin closed his eyes and called up the number "it's done."

This was a normal work day for her.

Five years earlier

Jasmin went out of the front door and started walking towards the lake where she was going to meet her *farfar* A green gray SUV is coming up slowly behind her and as she gets an uncomfortable feeling, she quickly decides to go down to a nearby trail in the woods along the lake. But the car doesn't stop following her. Three masked men get out of the car and run down the hill towards her. Jasmin started to run. As she ran, she turned her head to see where they were. She had gotten a good distance between her and her followers, but as she thought this, she trips on some roots that had grown from a nearby oak. She lost her balance and before she could get up or turn her head, it all went dark.

Chapter Two (the beginning of the start)

Present time:
She parks her car on the driveway of a white newbuild house, she is looking for her key in her purse when she hears someone say

"Hi Jasmin, does your aunt feel better?" It was her neighbor.

"Yeah, she loved your wool blanket."

Jasmin unlocks the door and is greeted by a wool blanket. She sighs and then takes a look around the house, nothing out of the ordinary. She took off her coat and walked up the stairs. She was having a warm long shower when her phone started to ring. "I just got home." she says to herself and lets it go to voicemail. She gets dressed and someone is calling her again.

"Where are you, what are you doing?" the voice asked.

"Robin, what do you want?"

"Well nothing, I just wanted to talk with you."

Jasmin is quiet.

"Can you be ready in two minutes?" asked Robin

"Do I even have a choice?" Jasmin said annoyingly

Outside her house is a black van and she opened the door. Robin says "drive" to the driver and they start to move.

"Did everything go well today?" He asks.

"Stop it already, what do you want? I have food that is waiting for me."

Robin looks at her.

Jasmin started to whine "Well you own me a pizza now."

Chapter Three (the uncovering)

Stockholm, Sweden

"Von Traufhsten is attending a charity gala tonight in 'Stora Salen'. You are going inside the east entrance, to the right you are going to see stairs only for employees, go up to the kitchen. You will put the nerve agent VX in his food." Robin explained

"Got it." said Jasmin as she put an earpiece in her ear

She had only used it one time before and it worked very well. Since it is easy to get the person to consume it and death is delayed. She started to chainching into staff clothes so she could go in unnoticed.

"Why? I'm just curious." Jasmin asked

"He wants to get into politics and is already buying up people, he wants corporations to decide everything basically." Robin said

The car stops and drops Jasmin off before parking on the street. She goes to the entrance and they let her in, not looking who she is. She thinks if they have this bad security something like this is bound to happen. Jasmin looked around. There were big beautiful chandeliers hanging from the second floor. She saw gorgeous dresses and for a moment she stopped and admired the women. But she had to force herself to go on, focus on the mission. She hurried up the stairs and she went inside the kitchen.

The food smelled really good, but it was warm and people were stressed.

She goes out through the doors and is greeted by AC and on the stage, a woman in a black and glittery pallet suit singing 'It's my party' by Lesley Gore. Behind her was a small orchestra. Jasmin looks at the tables so she would find where Von Traufhsten and his wife are seated. All she could do now was wait.

After 45 minutes it was finally time to take out the food. She finds the plates that are going to table 18 and discreetly put the poison in the food. The waitresses take out the plates and go to their respective tables. But the waitress doesn't stop at table 18 and keeps going further away. Jasmin can't see who is getting the food instead of Von Traufhsten but she knows she has to act fast.

As fast as she could she goes to the table and sees that it is Waleed Anderson that is going to take a bite of the food. She takes up a flower vase and spills it on him "Oh god I'm sorry, so so so sorry!" Waleed stands up and staff members are coming to help him. Jasmin takes away his plate and goes into a pantry.

"Robin, everything is wrong." she said very quietly

"What happened?"

"Someone is here."

"What are you talking about?" Robin asked

"Something's not right. Pick me up now, we have been compromised."

The van is rolling up to her and she gets in.

"What the hell..."Robin said

"Someone knew that we were gonna be there and who I was going to give it to. They gave the plate to the board member Waleed Anderson." said Jasmin

"That can't be a coincidence." Robin said

The driver turned his head and said "we are being followed."

"Pascal, lose them!"

Pascal completed his training in the Royal Air Force. He has an incredible resume and it was an easy choice for the organizations to hire him.

A few hours later Jasmin came home and walked in the kitchen where her frozen pizza was still waiting for her. She throws it away and takes out a new one from the freezer. She turned on the TV as she was standing and waiting at the microwave.

"A man has been declared dead after a car exploded. No one has claimed the attack and the police are not giving out any information at this time. Sources say it was the UK citizen charity foundation's creator Waleed Anderson. This has not been confirmed." she heard a reporter say

Jasmin takes a deep breath and says "who would do this?"

Chapter Four (the organization)

Five years earlier

She wakes up in a dark empty room. Her hands are tied behind her back with zip ties. She's looking for something to cut herself free with and after a few minutes she finds a sharp metal piece. Jasmin carefully saws in the plastic, after a while they break and she starts looking for a way out. The door doesn't have a handle. She started to press with her hands on the walls around the room, but realized quickly that there wasn't a way out. She starts to scream for help even though she doesn't know if anybody can hear her.

She sees blood on the floor and takes her hand to her head and she is bleeding from it. She is banging on the big gray door but no one comes. She had never felt so helpless before, nobody knew where she was. She had no idea why someone would do this to her. Jasmin sat on the floor for a long time, she didn't know how much time had passed and that it was cold. She looks at the door for a while and realizes that a screw is loose. She flies off the floor and starts to twist it with her hand. Her fingers start to bleed and she takes the metal piece and it finally comes out. She does the same thing with the last screw and she can take out the door hinge.

She starts to bang the door hinge against the walls. Her *farfar* always said "find the weakest spot" and this was exactly what she was doing. Jasmin finds it and starts to hit it till it becomes a little hole and starts to use her legs. She looks through it and sees a furnished room with the lights on. Her legs and arms were tired, but she refused to give up not now when she was this close. She got it big enough so she could press herself through it.

She doesn't believe what she sees, *farfar* with three other people standing looking at her.

"Good job Jesse!" said farfar

"New record." said another

Jasmin doesn't understand what is happening as she gets up off the floor her *farfar* hugs her and says "I knew you could do it."

"What, do what! What is this?" she can't get any words out.

Chapter Five (the beginning)

It has been a few days since the attack on Waleed and Jasmin goes through it in her head again and again. She must have missed something at the charity gala but what. How hard she tries she can't make sense of it.

"Oh glad you called Jasmin, I was just about to call you." Robin answered

"I want to talk about what happened, what we missed. Who had something to gain from his death." Jasmin said

"It was a rumor that he was going to be next in line for the chairman position, but nothing has been confirmed. So that is your job to find out. The chairman pointed you out to find the leek. He is sure it's one of the board members since no one else had that information."

"Why me?"

"He says he trusts you to be objective and you are one of the best in the field. Also you have only met three face to face Rue Cordova, Aaron Lane, and Ray Deacon."

"Understood." Jasmin said as she hung up

She goes up the stairs and takes one of her ready to go bags and goes out of the house. She meets up with Robin in a remote place where he gives her a file with pictures and names of all 13 members.

There are 12 board members and the chairman. Both old and young people from all around the world. It was the first time anyone had seen the full list like this who wasn't a board member.

Cruz Espinoza, 54 México
Jade Duran Toussaint 23, France
Ninos Ahmed 38, Syria
Waleed Anderson 79, Uk
Christian Vega 59, Germany
Ray Deacon 42, Australia
Kumar Chanin 19, India
Rue Cordova 25, South Afrika
Luke Myers 72, Us
Aaron Lane 51, Irland
Levi De Trier 28, Nederlands
Kwame Thette 86, Ghana
Conrad Haas 66, Switzerland

She was honored that she got to do this, they trusted her with this information. She is reading about everybody and their stories and what they have done for the organization. It was amazing to get to see it from this perspective, but she has to be objective. "Why would any of them kill Waleed?" she said quietly to herself

Chapter Six (the chairman)

Glace Bay, Nova Scotia, Canada
A few hours had passed and Jasmin was going to meet the chairman Luke Myrers in a parking lot in Glace Bay. Glace Bay has been a meeting place for the organization since it is a good location between Europe and North America.

Jasmin's hair and coat is blowing in the wind. She has black leader booths and a knee long light yellow dress. She used to say "If I'm going to die today I'm gonna do it with style." when people asked why she was wearing dresses and high heels. It wasn't the norm in this business to dress like her, sure she gets comments, but people don't suspect her as easily.

A car comes and stops right before her and a man gets out.

"Your reputation precedes you... You really do look like a killer queen." said a dark voice

"Mr Chairman, I'm honored to meet you." Jasmin said

"I have kept an eye on you, truly, truly special... Your work is something we haven't seen in years, its mind blowing... literally."

"Where do we start?" she asked

"I'm gonna give you more intel on everyone that you can read tonight in your warm and cozy cabin... and tomorrow a driver will pick you up at 9.20."

She got out of the car and started to walk towards the garden gate when she heard that someone was following her. She grabs a small knife as she had as a hairpin. She turns around and sees a shadow in the moonlight.

"I'm Kevin with the organization, take it easy. I work as a house sitter and guard this property. Esmeralda!" he said

Esmeralda is the codename for safehouses in this part of the world. She puts back her knife at its place and picks up her bag.

She opens the door and gets greeted by a big happy dog that walks over from the fireplace.

"This is Clifford, he is the real owner. He has been living here since he was a puppy. He knows what's up." said Kevin

Jasmin goes to her room and takes out all of the papers on the bed. She sits in an armchair and starts to read. She realizes that there's no intel on the chairman, Luke. "Why didn't he give his?" she said as she thought out loud.

Chapter Seven (Kumar Chanin)

She hastily woke up and looked at her phone: 7.32. She takes a deep breath and starts to read the files again. After a while she started to get ready, a dusty pink knee long dress and the same shoes as yesterday. Lastly she puts on her thigh holster and she is ready to go.

A white van picks her up and Jasmin asks where they are going.

"The plane." answers the driver

A man came and opened the door and gave Jasmin a phone and it was the chairman. "Kumar Chanin is in New Delhi, India." He hangs up before Jasmin could ask him about his file.

She landed at DEL and the safe house is relatively close to the airport. Jasmin is at the location where the safe house should be but she can't find where she is supposed to enter. It looks like someone put down concrete blocks without an entrance. She sees a small alleyway and goes to look closer and there are the stairs. Jasmin is searching for the right door and after a while she finds it. It was much better quality inside then it looked on the outside so she was more than happy. She takes off her holster, goes directly to the bed and sleeps since it should be an intensive day tomorrow.

She wakes up by a loud bang and she takes her gun and goes to the window. She sees that it was a few people packing things into a car outside. She breathes out and goes into the bathroom.

When she came out there was a man on her bed waiting for her.

"As you probably already figured out by now, I'm Kumar Chanin. The legend is true you do wear dresses and heels, interesting choice." he said

"Why are you here? How did you find me?" Jasmin asked

"I know a lot of things, but not who killed Waleed Anderson. I know you are here because of that and instead of you investigating me I want to help. He was a close friend to me, I would never kill him. I have nothing to gain from his death as you have read in your intel on me, no?" Kumar stated

"I personally don't suspect you, but I'm just doing what I'm told. You would do the same, if you really want to help let me check that you are good and then I can move on from you.

"I actually have a few things with me that I think would help. Do whatever you want, you know where to find me when you are ready." he said as he went out the door

She thinks for a second then rushes out the door and takes out her taser. He falls to the railing and she drags him inside and zip ties his hands to the radiator. She takes her purse and sees a bike outside leaning against a wall.

She is at Kumar's house and sees a guard sitting on the porch and is playing cards. She goes to him and asks where she is and he relaxes for a second. She tasered him and dragged him under a table. She can't kill him since he works for the organization.

She breaks a window and unlocks up the door from the inside. She thinks out of all people Kumar should have better security. Jasmin takes a look inside and nobody has cleaned in a long time. She looks in his drawers but she doesn't find anything she didn't already know. She sees a vase that has no dust on it and she picks it up. It's a key and she searches the room and sees a bookcase with a door on it. Inside it was a few books and she opened them and then a piece of paper falled down on the floor. It was a bunch of different coordinates and she put it in her purse.

The only places he has in India according to the organization are his mom and brother's places. Both of them were out so it was easy for her to check. She doesn't find any useful information in their place so she heads back.

A few minutes from the safe house she stops and sits on a stone, she looks up the coordinates and they are in the middle of nowhere all around the world.

Back in the apartment Kumar is still tied to the radiator and says "Finally what took you so long?"

"I was just being thorough and I did find a paper in a book with addresses, what are those?" Jasmin asked

"Waleed gave them to me a couple weeks ago, it was the last time I heard from him. I haven't been able to travel to them, I would guess it's a few different safe houses. It was actually a copy of that in the box I gave you. Remember?"

"Well I can't just take your word that this was everything now can I?"

There were a lot of documents about property and how to access banks when he was dead.

"How did you get this?" Jasmin asked

"It was just at my doorstep the day after he died. The security cameras show that it was some dude in a black hoodie placing it there. I don't know more about this than you do." Kamar said

Jasmin had no reason to not believe him at the moment, but why did Waleed leave it to Kumar and more importantly did he know he would get this when Waleed died.

Chapter Eight (Rue & Levi)

Jasmin was on her way to South Africa to meet with Rue Cordova. It was Rue and Levi de Trier who had concrete alibis. She had looked at every possibility and motive but she couldn't find any. They had been on an assignment with the organization the past two months and came home after Waleed was already dead. Jasmin can pick up on microexpressions and saw the video where they were told Waleed was dead and both were genuinely surprised.

She lands on Rue's own landing field outside Willowvale and a car came and picked her up. Rue owns a lot of land and has many houses on it. She had a lot of security but it was very discreet. When Jasmin came up to the main house Levi was already waiting outside.

"Hi, you must be Jasmin. Rue has told me so much about you." he said

"I hope it was good then." Jasmin laughs

"Come I'll show you to your room, Rue is in a meeting."

It was an open floor plan with a lot of flowers and modern art. They went up the stairs and to the left where a big wooden door stod open. It was a beautiful bed in the middle and a waterfall type thing with a tv over it. A big window with a view of a fireplace area. Jasmin thought "I could get used to this."

"Yours is so much nicer than mine anyway I'll let you get settled." Levi said and went into the door across the hallway

After a while the door opened and Rue came in and said "Jasmin I'm so happy to see you." while awkwardly giving her a hug

"Your meeting, what was that about?" Jasmin asked

"The chairman wanted to meet with all of the board members next week. He didn't say anything more, he's been acting very strange these last couple of days. Which is understandable but this is next level weird." Rue said

"How is he usually? I've never met him before this week."

"Nothing like he is now, I think dinner is almost ready. Do you want to join us?"

I do still love you my dear even though we broke
You made me feel like someone who could do anything by
your side and didn't have to swallow her pride
I still love you after all these lies

"You kept it even after all these years?"

Rue looked at her before walking down the stairs.

Down in the dining room they talked about past assignments and Levi and Jasmin got to know each other.

After a few hours they went down to the basement. It was a long hallway with dimmed lights, at the end it was a staircase leading up to a door.

They went up the stairs and through the door. It went up to Rue's office, it was a smaller house a few hundred meters from her main house. There were a few people looking at security cams and some were monitoring people.

"They have been watching every move since I got the news. Shall we get started?" Rue asked and clapped her hands together.

The three of them sat down at a desk and started a process of elimination.

Chapter Nine (the meeting)

Levi and Rue got an invitation to a meeting with the charman and the board.

Lofthouse, Harrogate, North Yorkshire, England
Friday 15.00 local time, outside crown

It was Wednesday and they are not close to finding any evidence against people who knew their protocols. They needed to make a plan to get intel on the chairman.

Rue and Jasmin took a walk along the estate and talked about old times in boot camp where they met and their relationship when Rue got a phone call. She looked worried.

"What? Who was it?" Jasmin asked

"It was security, they had seen someone climbing over the gate. Not the first gate, this gate." Rue said

Jasmin lifted up her dress a little and took a knife out of the thigh holster she had on. Rue had a gun on her ankle and released the safety. They walked slowly towards the gate and they saw four men throwing over bags.
Rue whispered "guards should be here soon."

A car approached the men and they started shooting the driver. Rue took a shot and hit one of them in the head.

The men started in Rue and Jasmin's direction. They took cover against a few stones. Jasmin looked up and saw that everybody in the car was on the ground.

"Shit, they are coming!" she said

Rue took another shot but missed. They were returning fire and Jasmin had to think fast. She took her knife and threw it in one of their legs. She had two more, but she missed one and the other one of the men got in his neck.

"I'm all out." said Jasmin

"I've only got one bullet left."

As they got ready for a fight they heard two shots from a different gun and someone said "It's safe."

They looked up and saw that it was Levi who had run as fast as he could.

"Where are the other guards? You have more than these five, right?" asked Jasmin

"They are ordered to defend the house and office at all costs, too much valuable information is stored there and I can take care of myself. These men must have killed my poor workers who live down by the first gate."

"Who are they? Why are they here and how did they find your house?" Levi asked

"I don't know, it must be related to Waleed's death. This has never happened before. We are doing security threats every single day. It really is someone from the organization, I didn't want to think that one actually could betray us. It's only the board members who know everything, my security is vetted, workers don't know anything about my work and they are also carefully picked out and vetted." she said

"I'm gonna call Pascal so he can pick us up for that meeting. Should probably tell Robin also." Jasmin said

"Can we trust them?" asked Rue

"Yes, I work with him very closely and I did check that he was good when I first heard the news." said Jasmin

A few hours later they were on the plane and started to go over their plan again.

"Jasmin you are gonna sit outside with a stroller while Levi and I meet the others. Levi is going to wear a camera in his glasses and a better microphone than what it is in the earpieces. Then you Jasmin take this wig on and get an excuse to come close to us." Rue explained

Chapter Ten (the woman and the doll)

They landed at LBA in Leeds and Pascal had a car waiting for them. It smelled rain in the air but it was sunny. They drove about 50 minutes until they came to a small village called Lofthouse.

Pascal dropped Jasmin off a few hundred meters before the meeting place and she took out the stroller from the trunk. She took out the life-like doll and put it in the stroller. Pascal drove away and dropped Rue and Levi in front of the crown. Jasmin walked over to a bench and took her computer that was hidden in the stroller.

After a while a gray van came and four came out. It was Cruz Espinoza, Jade Duran Toussaint, Ray Deacon and Christian Vega and they greeted Rue and Levi. Jasmin looked at her phone. It was 14.48, not too long now. The others were talking about Waleed just in general. One car came and two men got out, it was Kwame Thette and Conrad Haas. A man got out of a building and it was Luke Myers, the chairman he was already here. Ninos Ahmed and Kumar Chanin joined shortly after but no sign of Aaron Lane.

"It's time we can wait any longer, he can catch up with us later." said the chairman

All of them went inside the crown and Jasmin turned up the volume so she could hear what they said. She took a deep breath and brightened the screen on the computer.

"As you all know, we have a situation. It was one we all knew could happen. We accepted the risks, but we were betrayed by one of our own.... One who knows about our operation in detail and that leaves us in this room." said the chairman who sat on the short side of the long table.

Everybody started to look around at each other, but Levi and Rue both looked at the chairman.

He continued "We must find the mole at all costs. You need to give me your locations for the last 3 months.... Don't think even for a second that you can hide anything from me, from us. I have a person who already checked all of you so even the smallest mistake in your history will have consequences. We will go where the evidence leads us."

They looked frightened as they started to write down everywhere they have been. Jasmin saw the look on Jade and Conrad's face, it was worse than the others. But it could have something to do with them being Primary and Secondary Minute Takers. They have to take notes and write their own location. Jasmin looked up from her computer and let her eyes wander. Aaron Lane had still not showed up.

She began looking at flight records, no sign of any of his aliases. She needed Rue to get the chairman's phone, but she also needed to look where Aaron was. She got up from the bench and started walking towards the door. She had to come up with an excuse fast. She had already seen in which room they were in but she needed a reason and Kumar had already seen her before as a few others. She took a vacuum cleaner and started to move to the room. She had a black wig on her and heavy makeup.

"Housekeeping!" Jasmin said outside the door.

"Busy, don't disturb." said a voice, she guessed it was the chairman.

She opened the door and said "I'm sorry, but I gotta clean you know." with a heavy British accent."My shift is about to end. You know what I mean, I won't be long. Don't worry I will be out of your hair soon, love."

They all sat in silence and waited for Jasmin to get out but she needed to get his phone somehow.

"Darling, you have something under your chair. If you could be an angel and move a little bit." she said

Jasmin pushed Rue gently closer to the chairman and began to crawl under the table. She said "Oh my goodness, it's pork here. Someone has left pieces here. We apologize."

She got to the chairman's feet and put a small tracking device under his shoe, but it fell off. "I'm sorry, busy day you know. Rubbish anyone, I can take it with me."

"Here." said Rue and gave Jasmin a napkin and tinfoil curled up in a big ball.

"Thank you, love." Jasmin said.

Jasmin closed the door behind her and let out a quiet little laugh. She took the ball and flattened it out. There was a phone, she needed to return it before he knew it was missing. She got to her stroller and copied the phone. She looked at the latest call numbers and it was to Aaron. He had talked to him but didn't say anything.

Chapter Eleven (time is not on our side)

She started to plan her way back into the room. Nothing that makes sense and does not ruin her cover. She got downstairs to the stroller and took out a plastic bag. In it was a new look, she now had a short light blond wig and a bright red vest with blue jeans.

"This is the most ugly thing I've ever seen."Jasmin said quite

She went out of the bathroom and up the stairs again. She had a form and some papers with her. She opened the door to the meeting room.

"Oh, I didn't know anyone was here. I will be quick." she said with a southern american accent.

The chairman placed his head in his hands and just sighed. Jasmin started to walk around the room and pretend she had something to inspect. She dropped the phone in the back of Levi's chair. Then she said to the chairman "Move, I gotta check on the vent."

He did what she said mostly because no one talked to him like that. Levi got up and said "Do you need any help?" and dropped Luke's phone in his pocket.

"Nah, I'm on my way." Jasmin said as she was on her way out the door.

"What is even happening... I asked for complete privacy and this is how they treat us... Where were we?" said the chairman

"I have a question. Why is Aaron still not here? Has anybody heard from him?" asked Jade

"No I haven't." said Kumar

"Me neither." agreed Kwame

"Should we worry?" asked Christian

"Yeah, Waleed is already dead so we should definitely try to contact him" said Ninos

"Enough! You all know better than to worry. I have people looking into his whereabouts... If he is hiding then he has a good reason for it." the chairman said

Everyone sat quiet and looked at each other.

Chapter Twelve (the house on the cliff)

"That went somewhat good, don't you think." said Rue

"If you mean horribly then yes." said Jasmin

"Well she said somewhat good, not good." Pascal said from the driver seat.

"He definitely suspected something, nothing I did was remotely normal." Jasmin said as she breathe out

They got on a very small plane where Robin stood and waited for them. Pascal started it up and they flew a little while. The plane landed on a private airfield in the middle of nowhere, they got out and Pascal took off again.

It was a relatively new house and the security was the best on the market. Jasmin's *farfar* had built it after he got recruited to the organization. The house was built together with the surroundings. It was the most remote place you could find. He used to say "I want to know when someone is coming to knock on my door so I can pretend I'm not home." When she first got recruited she finally got it, "know where your enemies are before they even know it."

They all went up to the entrance and Levi said "Sea view, not bad."

"Just wait until you actually are at the lookout point." Robin said

Jasmin opened the door and was welcomed by two dogs. "You home!" Jasmin shouted

"Yes and now deaf thanks to you." a middle aged woman said.

"Charlotte! It's been way too long. How is everything?"

"Never been better. Let's show the guests their rooms. Alrighty follow me." Charlotte said.

They went upstairs to the conference room so they could talk in private.

"Who the hell is she?" Rue said

"My lover obviously." Jasmin said sarcastically as she went to start the projector.

"Charlotte is her live-in house sitter and the dogs are Jasmin's if you were wondering. Krystall and Nessie." said Robin

"When you think you know someone." Rue said disappointed

"Okay let's begin before they start more drama." said Levi

They looked at the time line once again. "We know for a fact that Rue, Kamar and Levi did not do this. So the question is: Where is Aaron? What is the chairman hiding? Who is the next person in line for the board? I'm thinking that Levi and Rue know this." Jasmin said

"There were multiple candidates but I don't think it really matters who was at the top." Rue stated

"Ehh yes it does, for the love of all gods just say it. Stop with all this bureaucratic shit." said Jasmin annoyingly

Levi hesitates before he says "Robin."

"I swear I had no idea about this. Believe me I wouldn't kill someone for that. I'm happy where I'm." Robin said

Jasmin is looking out of a window and says "I've known Robin for a long time, if he did it he probably would have told me. Who else was on that list?"

"Only him." Rue said

"No no no, you seriously can't believe this. So that is what people think of me now. I plan things, sitting behind a screen I don't..." Robin said as he got up and shut the door.

Chapter Thirteen (the organization II)

Five years earlier
Farfar explained that he works for the organization and that it is a network across the world. It started with the help of about forty countries and their main function is to keep peace in as many countries as possible. It doesn't matter who gets hurt, it is for the greater good.
"You said that you worked as a rifleman in the military." Jasmin asked confused

"I did that for a few years till the organization recruited me." he explained

"So why am I here?"

"Because I have always seen potential in you, I've trained you for this all your life Jesse. You are the most extraordinary, intelligent, funniest person I know. Not only that but your physical performance is remarkable." *farfar* said

"We have followed your progress and it's hard to find one young sophisticated woman." a man agreed

"You still have a lot to learn but you are definitely ready."

Jasmin sits down on a chair to take in what just had happened. How could she not have known her own grandfather was a hitman. He had been so normal and nice, a completely normal *farfar* to her.

She gets up and goes to the door. The man moves away and she leaves the room. She tries to find a way out but it's only corridors with doors everywhere.

She finally sees a glassdoor and it is people inside who are moving around. Jasmin goes closer and can see a lot of screens, she opens the door slowly and looks around. It was the latest technology.

Someone put their hand on her shoulder and said "You could work here."

She has so many questions, she doesn't know where to start. She turned around and asked "Where are we?"

"We are on a blacksite, you will get to know more once you start your training here." *farfar* said

But she didn't know what to say to that. A few hours ago they kidnapped her and now they want her to work here.

"Why would I want that?" she asked

"I know that you want this, I see myself in you. You would be a brilliant addition to the team."

It is true what he says and she has always wanted to do something like this, something bigger than herself.

"It's wrong to kill innocent people." she said

"Everyday innocent people die and get hurt for no reason. Everything we do has a bigger meaning to it for the greater good, the end justifies the means. It's going to be collateral damage but so is it with everything in life. What we do here saves many more lives than what we take." *farfar* said

Jasmin thinkes for a while and then says "Fine, I think about it."

Chapter Fourteen (the fight)

Rue looked over the same papers again and again. It all looked like Robin was the one who had most to gain from Waleed's death. Especially on the money front, he had a big loan and him being on the board would give him a lot more money.

"Jasmin, I'm sorry but look at these." Rue said as she handed the papers over

"I checked him out, he's good. As soon as I came home that night, I looked up everywhere he had been over the past two months and his phone records from a year back . Nothing that is wired or out of the ordinary." said Jasmin

"Burner phone." said Rue

"Yeah, I know. But why? Why? I know him, he would never do this and definitely not expect to get away with it. It doesn't make sense." Jasmin said

"Stop it, never ever let emotions take over or decide. It's literally the first thing they taught us." Levi said

It was quiet for a while and then Rue went down to the dogs. She threw a ball a couple of times on the small lawn just outside the house and she heard a car driving and turned around. She could see a few more coming down on the road. Rue went inside and screamed "Cars!"

Jasmin and Levi who were still sitting in the room got up and went to a window and she said "Ah, shit!"

"Rue, dogs and Charlotte safe room now. Levi, weapons!" said Jasmin as she pointed in the direction of the weapon safe.

Levi handed over guns, grenades and a rifle to Jasmin and a shotgun to Robin. Charlotte closed the door to the safe room, where she could watch it unfold on security cameras. Rue pushed over a table to a window so she could lay down and get a good view of the property.

"Who the hell are they, it is only we who know we are here." said Jasmin

"I'm telling you, it's Robin." Levi said

This time Jasmin went quiet and didn't disagree.

"They are in range!" Rue shouted from the dining room.

"Shoot them!" said Jasmin and Levi in agreement

Robin, who was not particularly experienced in combat, hid behind a chair. He was ready to shoot anyone who walked through the front door.

Meanwhile Rue had taken down four soldiers already. Jasmin had gone to take a look over the sea to see if she saw a boat or something moving, but she didn't.

The soldiers had found out where the bullets came from and hid behind trees to get to a better position. They had a few long gunners but Rue had the advantage since she had the higher ground.

A window broke besides Levi and he got down on the floor and crawled towards Robin.

"This was all you, I just can't figure out how or when."

"Not me, I've told you already. I don't gain anything from this." said Robin defencive
Levi just shook his head and said "I should just kill you right now!"

Before Robin got a chance to react, Jasmin opened the front door and threw a grenade at the soldiers. She closed the door just as fast and grabbed a revolver. She grabbed a knife from her left leg and waited till Rue said "Now!"

She was ready for them and the door opened and Robin shot the man which gave Jasmin the advantage of element of surprise. She stabbed one of them in the lower arm and used his body as a shield while slitting his throat.

Levi had gotten up and was right behind Jasmin. He tapped on her shoulder and said "ready, go!" She threw away the soldiers body and shot one of them right below the eye and Levi got a headshot. They didn't see anyone so they took cover.

"Rue, how's it looking?" asked Jasmin

"I got one running and the rest are still behind the trees hiding."

Meanwhile Charlotte is sitting on the edge of the chair watching intensely. There were a lot of different buttons, but she didn't know what they did. She saw one 'deploy outside' and she saw the soldiers behind the tree and before even thinking about it she pressed it.

"They are heading this..." before Rue could finish her sentence, landmines blew up all around the property.

"The hell was that!?" Levi asked

Robin, Jasmin and Levi looked at each other and then outside the window. There was not much left of the soldiers or the landskap.

"That takes care of it." Rue said as she walked to the others

"Who... Who did that?" Jasmin asked

"I did." said someone behind them

"What, how? What! eh." Levi said shooked. "I thought you were normal."

Rue hit Levi and gave him the stop expresion with her face.

"Incoming!" Robin said

"What no, no, no, no, no!" Charlotte said as she ran towards the safe room again.

Just above the water a helicopter flew. They got ready for another fight and someone called Jasmin. She answered and a familiar voice said "Don't worry it's me your savior, get out."

"It's Pascal, hold fire."

Chapter Fifteen (the half truth)

"Charlotte, time to get out help is here. Take the dogs with you." Jasmin shouted

Everyone got their things and started to head down the cliff. Pascal had gone out of the helicopter and said "Man I'm the best aren't I."

"How did you know we needed help?" Rue asked suspiciously

"Robin sent a weird message so I thought I would check on you."

"See Robin has nothing to do with Waleed." Jasmin said

"Or maybe this was his plan all along." Levi said

They took off and landed on an airfield a few towns away. Pascal had left his plane there.

"Where are we going?" Charlotte asked

"You are going to a safe house. I'm gonna go find a car." Jasmin said

She found an old car without any GPS and hot wired it. Charlotte put the dogs in the back and her stuff in the trunk.

"You guys wait here, I'll be back soon." Jasmine said

"Wait, can I...uh you know?" Rue stuttered

"Yes, get in the back."

There wasn't much space left but Rue managed to get in and they drove away.

Pascal and Robin started to talk and Levi came up to them and said "Pascal how can you talk with this traitor."

"You need to let it go, okay got it." Pascal said

"So you are on his side, wait till I tell the chairman this. You are not gonna have a job for long."

Pascal just shook his head and said "some things are not even worth responding to."

"Why do you hate me so much, what have I ever done to you. I just saved your life so you are welcome." Robin defended himself

"Traidor, that's what you are!" Levi said angrily as he walked away

"Well he is somewhat right though, isn't he? I know you know more than you're letting on." Pascal said

Jasmin, Rue and Charlotte were driving on a small dirt road when Charlotte asked "What is the deal with you two anyway?"

"What do you mean?" Rue answered

"I think you know what I'm talking about?"

"We were just sisters in arms in boot camp, nothing interesting." Jasmin said

"Wow so now I'm nothing interesting, that hurts." Rue said

"You said past tense 'were' what happened?"

"Fell out of touch." Jasmin answered

They got to a little cabin surrounded by trees and bushes. A creek was beside the garden and it looked like it was abandoned.

"Welcome, to you new home for a while." said Jasmin

"It looks scary." Charlotte said

"Nah it has electricity, water and everything you need and no one will find you. You are gonna be safe here and here is a phone, someone will call you in a few days. Also

give you a car and some food. You will be taken care of."
Jasmin reassured her

Charlotte looked at Jasmin and asked "Who owns it?"

"Me actually, well technically 'Elizabeth Martin'" said
Rue "Jasmin and I lived here for a year."

They unpacked the car and Jasmin and Rue said goodbye
to Charlotte, Krystall and Nessie. Charlotte was standing
on the patio and waved as they drove away.

"Friends, yeah right."she said to herself

Back at the airfield, Pascal got the plane ready and Robin
was talking on the phone. Levi came back to the plane
when he saw the car come back.

"Where are we going now?" Levi asked Rue and Jasmin

"Here." Jasmin said as she pointed at the coordinates she
had gotten from Kumar.

Chapter Sixteen (the coordinates)

They changed planes to another plane that had a longer reach and landed at LYS in Lyon, France where a few of the coordinates were. They got a car and drove to the place which was a warehouse.

"Okay, okay interesting." Rue said with a funny voice while Jasmin was laughing at her

They got out of the car and took out their weapons except Robin who sat and waited in the car. Rue and Jasmin took the front door while Pascal and Levi got around the back. Rue kicked the wooden door in and Jasmin realized that it was open and said "personally I would just open the door but your way works too."

"Shut up!" Rue said jokingly

It was completely empty on the inside and Pascal and Levi met up with them. Rue saw some cables laying on the floor and picked them up.

"So someone has been here, that something at least." Jasmin said

"Guys cameras." Pascal said

"Oh shit, get out." Levi said

"It was one more location nearby, wasn't it?" Levi asked

"Robin, show Pascal were." Jasmin said

They drove for ten minutes and saw an abandoned school, but this time there were cars parked outside.

"I think you'll have better luck with this one." Robin said

They all got out of the car once again and looked around to see if they could enter the building undetected. Robin had a thermal camera ready and said "it's two people who are moving around upstairs and about seven sitting still. No one on the first floor that I can see. Proceed with caution."

Jasmin checked the door handle and it was locked. She pointed to the window besides the door and Levi took out his glass breaker. "They are gonna notice this so Pascal you cover us out here." said Jasmin

He gave them a nood and Levi broke the glass. Robin saw on the thermal camera that one of the two people moved down the stairs. "Movement, incoming." Robin said in the earpiece

They walked in slowly and cleared the rooms on the first floor. The guard came down and Jasmin was waiting on them, she had a silencer on her gun and she shot him in the neck. It was suppressed but it's not quite so the other guard would hear it and come down which he did.

This time Rue hit him in the head with the back of her gun so they could intergait him later. Both guards had rifles and handguns. "Now this is something." Rue said

They walked up the stairs and they came into what seemed like an office. "Up with your hands now, if we see someone moving we are going to shoot first then ask." Levi said

"What are you doing here, trust me when I say you want to be truthful with me. The alternative is not gonna be pretty." said Jasmin

"Now tell us, what are you doing and who are you working for?" Rue continued

"We gather intel, we are nobody. Please don't hurt us, I have three kids." said a worker

"Who... Are... You... Working... For!" Levi shouted

"We don't know, we never meet the boss. I promise you." said another man

Levi, Rue and Jasmin looked at each other, to try to determine their statements. "Well you get your orders from somewhere." Rue said

"A man, he said this would be risk free. He comes once a month." said a woman crying.

Jasmin went out of the room and called the chairman. "We need transport and clean up for eight people, one dead. I will send you the coordinates."

"How did you... get this number?" he asked

"By doing my job even when they don't give me their file." Jasmin said and hung up

"Okay, let's go. Put him in the back of the car, we are going to have a little chat." Jasmin said and pointed at the guard who was still alive

Back at a safe house Rue saw that he started to wake up.

"Had a nice sleep?" Rue asked the guard

He looked confused around and tried to get out of the chains he was locked to.

"I'm sorry that won't work, I'm afraid, so I'll ask you only one time. Who do you work for?" Rue said

"*Quelle... connasse.*" he said

"Okay you are going to wish you talked to me, bring her in." said Rue

Jasmin walked into the room in a red evening gown and said "Do you like it? I like it."

The guard started to laugh and said "Is this your idea of scary or something? A pretty little lady that wouldn't even hurt a fly. Can't probably not even use a weapon if a man doesn't show her."

"Oh we are going to have some fun aren't we. Give me my stuff." Jasmin said

"Your stuff is probably a makeup brush since that is the only thing you can do." he said

"I know you are trained for this stuff so I'm not going to bother and I wouldn't want to ruin my dress because of you. We will do this my way, the right way."

He looked at her with fear for the first time on his face. She took out a box with a black cover on it and took a deep breath and said "Funny you mentioned flys, you are going to get to know them a lot better."

She drags the cover off and hundreds of flies are flying around. She puts the box over his head and leaves it there for a few minutes. She is talking with Levi about Jade since Jade is from France.

"Her brother died two years ago in an accident. It affected her very much." Levi said

"I read that in her file, how did he die?" Jasmin asked

"He fell down hiking, they say he tripped or something."
Rue answer

"Who are they?"

"The organization." Levi said

Jasmin started to say something, but the man screamed
so she went to check on him.

"Are you ready to talk now, or should we leave you here
overnight?" Jasmin said

"Okay look all I know is that it's some rich dude okay, he
is funding this." He said

"Now we are going somewhere, tell me about yourself
and who gives you orders."

"Okay I'm Sebastian, I live here in France and some rich
dude."

"Yeah but who gives you orders? You know what, this
goes back on" Jasmin said as she put the box over his
head again.

 She waited a few more minutes and took it off. "His
name is Benjamin. I have his number in my phone, please
don't put it on again." Sebastian begged

"Oh no don't worry, it's all over now." She said as she pulled out her gun and shot him from a distance.

Levi took out Sebastian's phone and held his thumb to the fingerprint scanner.

"Robin, you can come in now, trace this number. Give me everything you find. I'm going out for a while.

Chapter Seventeen (the other guy)

Jasmin was standing outside a car and talking on the phone with Kumar who had been to other locations.

"Jasmin, the bank account it's not Waleed's. I can't get access to them. But they have a lot of money in it like a lot."

"Where are you now, should we meet up? I'm in Lyon, France."

"I was headed towards Russia, but I will tell the pilot to turn around."

"Good, see ya." Jasmin said before she hung up.

Robin told Rue that Benjamin lived in central Lyon. Rue and Levi went out to ask Jasmin if she wanted to go with them.

"Well yeah, what." she answered very confused

Rue threw the keys to Jasmin and they got in the car.

"Why did she get to drive? I never get to drive?" Levi asked

"She can actually drive unlike you." Rue defended her

They got into the city and tried to find his apartment.

"Oh look, Rue, your name is on every street." Levi said

"It literally means street in french." Jasmin explained

"Here I think, fifth floor." Rue said from the passenger seat

They got out of the car and went to find the door up to the apartment. Inside they looked at every door on the fifth floor to find the right one. Jasmin knocked on the door and someone opened it.

"Bonjour, I'm looking for Benjamin. Is he here?"

"Who is asking?" the man said with a heavy french accent

"Oh yes of course, I'm Tess and a friend said he had my wallet." Jasmin said

"I don't have your wallet." he answer

"Is there someone else in there, they said you had it and gave this address."

"No only me."

Levi who had stood behind the door pushed him into the apartment, he tried to close the door but Rue held on to it. They went inside and zip tied him to the kitchen counter.

"Who are you?" he asked terrified

"Someone that has the power over you now, it can be quick or painful your choice." said Jasmin

"My advice is do what she says and it'll be painless." Rue said

"Who do you work for? Really think about it and say the right thing."

"For a restaurant." he said with a calm voice

"You gotta be kidding me." Jasmin said and looked at Levi who took out his gun and pointed it at Benjamin.

"Remember now?" Levi asked

"A restaurant, I promise you."

"I don't like being lied to." Jasmin said as she took out one of her knives and pushed it against his liver. He didn't say anything so she forced it in between his ribs.

"Okay, yes I don't work for a restaurant."

She turned it around and he screamed "A woman. The other guy was much nicer than you."

"Progress, that is good. Which guy?" Jasmin said

"Who gives you orders?" Rue asked

"A woman."

Jasmin looked him in the eye and started to pull out the knife.

"Fine, fine she has brown hair and is being called 'Blanc' white in french. That's all I know. I swear." he said against his will

"The other guy?" Jasmin asked again

"He had a British accent. He didn't say who he was. Please, I have told you everything."

"Okay nice to meet you." Jasmin said as she took another knife and stabbed him in his neck.

"Levi, can you take out my knives? I don't want blood on this dress." she said as Benjamin slowly bled out

They closed the door behind them and she once again called the Chairman "Clean up, I will send you the address."

"What are you doing? Why are you calling me in the middle of the night" the chairman said angrily

"Tell me what you know and I'll stop." she said

He didn't answer so she said "Call you soon then, bye."

"You can't seriously be calling the chairman, no one does that. On rare occasions he will call you and that's it." Rue said

"Well he should have known better then to assign me to this then, shouldn't he?" Jasmin answered

Her phone vibrated and she picked up it was Kumar who said he had landed and needed a pick up. "I'll tell Pascal."

Chapter Eighteen (he is back)

Kumar had already arrived at the safe house. It was very quiet when the three of them walked in.

"Okay what do you know? Tell us everything and we will do the same." Rue asked

"I have been to a few of the places Waleed gave me and there were servers everywhere. In Italy there was an office that had been cleared out. I was on my way to check out the one in Russia but you called, so I came here." Kumar said

"We have also been at an office and warehouse, but it was people inside. Long story short a man named Sebastian takes orders from Benjamin who works for a woman who works for a rich man. At least that is the theory at the moment." Jasmin said

"And Benjamin said it was another guy with a British accent who had asked questions." Levi contributed

"Oh shit so Waleed has been here or Aaron he is Irish right?" Kumar asked

"Yes but they don't sound the same." said Pascal quietly to Kumar

"We believe that those things could be related but we don't know. I don't jump to conclusions. I feel like Jade would have known he had been here though. She didn't say anything at the meeting." said Jasmin

"Conrad also, He lives in switzerland." Kumar said

"He was on an assignment in Japan, at the time. Before and after Waleed was murdered."

"Jade?"

"She was in the US at the time of his death and before she was home." Jasmin said and it clicked "You said before, her brother, accident." she continued

Robin took his computer out of his bag and said "It was two years anniversary of his death I think, she was home here in France the whole month before Waleed's death."

"Wait, we can't accuse her of anything, just because she lost her brother." Rue said

They all looked at her and then at each other.

"Here is a news article." Robin said

Last Wednesday morning the French Ambassador Mrs. Sylvie Toussaint's husband was found deceased. Lyle Toussaint's

body was discovered by a group of hikers, officials say "It was a terrible accident."

One of the hikers who was at the scene said "He had fallen from the hiking trail with his bike and landed on a rock" This has however not been confirmed by the investigators at this point of time. His autopsy showed no signs of foul play according to the authorities.

His funeral will be held later this month in his hometown. On Thursday Mrs. Toussaint announced her leave of absence. She will return to France with her late husband.

Mr. Toussaint was survived by his wife and sister.

"So what was the cause of death?" Jasmin asked

"Blunt force trauma to the head. Well the official report said that. But when Jade first told us she said it wasn't an accident and they covered it up."

"A few months later she said it was an accident and then she said didn't think clearly and asked us to stop looking into it." Kumar said

"But why would anyone want to kill him to begin with?" Robin asked

"She said then it was to get his wife out of the county, but the chairman said it was an accident and we have no reason to suspect the organization of lying." Rue said

They all went and tried to get some sleep, but with a job like this it can sometimes be hard to relax.

The next morning Jasmin got up and put on a black and white dress with black over knee boots.

"Looking good!" said Kumar when Jasmin walked into the main area.

"Always" she answered

Levi and Rue were still sleeping, Robin had made breakfast and Pascal went out for a run.

"We have forgotten about Aaron, do you know where he can be? Any motive to kill Waleed?" Jasmin asked Kumar

"No idea, apparently you don't know people as well as you think you do." he answers

"Have you talked to him before he disappeared?"

"Now that you are saying it. Right after Waleed died he said that it was someone from the board."

"Where the hell is he then?" Jasmin said as she put down a plate

Chapter Nineteen (the bank)

It had started to rain and they gathered around the car.

"We need to meet the chairman, he knows where Aaron could be." Levi said

"How are we supposed to do that?" Rue asked

Jasmin had already picked up her phone and called him.

"Yes." he answered with a sigh

"What do you know about Aaron Lane? Where is he? What was he doing? But most importantly, why did you leave out Jade's dead brother?" she asked

"To see if you'd find it...which you have. Aaron Lane is off the grid, not on my orders... I have not spoken to him since before Waleed Anderson's death." he answered

Jasmin looked at the other and the words "he called him, the meeting before it."

"You think this is funny, I don't like when people lie to me." she said and hung up

Rue, Levi and Kumar looked shocked at Jasmin.

"You are so dead, he will kill you the first opportunity he gets."

They all got in the car except Kumar and drove to one of the banks where Waleed's killer had an account.

"Bonjour, we would like to get access to the security cameras." Jasmin said with a smile on her face

"Can't do that madam."

Rue took the gun out slightly and the receptionist let them in.

"Thank you!" Jasmin said

Rue disabled the cameras and Robin took the harddrive. The receptionist reached for a silent alarm, Levi shot her before she could press it and everyone except Levi and Jasmin walked out of there. They were going to stay and clean up while Rue got some materials for them. In the car Robin let the face scanning software search for Aaron and Waleed. He got a match for Waleed and a few day's later Aaron. "Rue, Aaron was following Waleed. We have actual physical evidence this time."

Meanwhile at the bank Levi got a phone call. He answer it and the voice said "Authentication code."

"523892"

"Levi, would you tell Jasmin that Von Traufhsten has moved his event up till tonight in Besançon instead of the day after tomorrow." said the chairman

"How do you even know I'm with her?" Levi asked

"Robin"

"Robin what?"

Jasmin looked concerned at Levi

"Yes... he told me when I called him."

"You called Robin? Why?"

"Intel that Von Traufhsten is in France."

"When?"

"When you... were in the UK. He didn't tell you."

"Thank you Mr. Chairman." Levi said and hung up

"What was that all about?" asked Jasmin

"Robin told the chairman that we all were together and not only that but he knew Von Trafsten was in France and he did not tell us." Levi said agitated "By the way we are going to an event tonight in Besançon."

Jasmin didn't say anything and immediately went back to cleaning. Rue came back with supplies and they told her what they knew about Robin. They took the body with them back to the car and told Pacal they needed to be in Besançon.

"Around a three hour drive." Pascal said as he read from his phone

Chapter Twenty (Besançon)

"Why? Where is it even?" asked Robin

"Von Traufhsten is there." Jasmin answered

Robin nodded his head and looked down then away.

"I feel like this is not the dress code for this event."
Jasmin said

"You literally couldn't look more gorgeous, professional
or fit in better anywhere. Robin, can you tell us what the
occasion is?" Rue said

"Why would I know?"

"Don't even start with that, you tell us now or else we are
gonna have a bigger problem. You understand?" said Levi

"Robin honestly, we know that you know. The chairman
told us, so stop it already. I have really been trying to stay
on your side and then you hide stuff like this from us. So
you better start telling the truth about this, I don't like
being lied to." said Jasmin

"It is a launch party." he responded

"Well I can't go in like this." Rue said

"I got you covered and you too Levi or at least partly." Jasmin said and laughed

Rue and Levi looked at each other and then back at Jasmin.

"I know neither of you do dresses so I have this ready everywhere." she continued

She held up two shirts and fabric.

"You still do that." Rue said emotionally

"Let the fabric do the magic!" Jasmin said with an dramatic voice

Jasmin tried not to poke Rue with needles. When it was ready Rue asked Jasmin to take a picture so she could see how she looked.

"This is amazing, you are amazing."

Jasmin had cut the black shirt vertically so it looked like a tassel on the arms and a normal white t-shirt that she had taken off one of the arms. So it went diagonally across her collarbone to the chest.

They were a few streets away from the citadel when they put their earpieces in and did a sound check.

"Rue" said Robin

"Yeah"

"Jasmin" he continued

"Yes"

"Levi"

"Unfortunately"

"Pascal"

"Uie"

"Okay good to go." Robin confirmed

They got out of the car and Robin said "Wait, do you think his security knows what you guys look like."

"That's why we go together and Jasmin alone. They don't know her so we won't blow her cover." Rue answered

"And that is why I'm the guy behind the screen."

"Pascal, don't let him leave your sight." Levi said

"Yes boss."

Levi, Rue and Jasmin were walking around and tried to find a car that would match everybody else's.

"Here." Rue said

Levi waited for the driver to lock the car so he could copy the radio waves then he took out his fob. He got in the driver seat and said "Finally, I get to drive!"

"Don't even think about driving 'the Levi way' and come straight back here when you drop her off." Rue said

"I keep no promises." he said as he speed away

He drove up to the entrance and got out of the car and opened the back door for Jasmin. She got out on the blue carpet leading up the stairs. A waiter came up to her with a salver and Jasmin took a glass of champagne and went inside.

Levi drove away and went to pick up Rue who stood and waited where he had left her. It was a car before him who had stopped in the intersection and Levi was getting impatient. After a minute he got out of the car and approached the driver who was talking on the phone. He screamed "What is wrong with you?"

The driver did not answer and Levi continued to attempt to get the driver to move.

Rue was looking at her watch and said "Levi, where are you?"

"Go on your own." he answered

She started to go towards the citadel when she heard sirens but she didn't think much of it and went up the stairs to find a place she could sneak in. Meanwhile Jasmin was going around listening to the orchestra and looking at the beautiful architecture when she saw von Traufhsten and his wife.

"Excuse me, I just wanted to thank you for this amazing evening so far." Jasmin said as she almost tripped "Thank you! I wish I could take the credit for it but it's mostly my wife's work." von Traufhsten answers

"Well it's lovely!" she said and looked at his wife

"I appreciate it, I assume we can count on you?" she said

"Absolutely!" Jasmin answered and they went on their way.

Rue had just made it inside and said "I'm in. Jasmin, where are you?"

"At the fountain."

"A fountain! Man, sometimes I wish I wasn't behind the screen." Robin said

"Keep it clear!" Pascal said to Robin in a direct voice

Rue met up with Jasmin and they started planning how they should get von Traufhsten out of there.

"He is going to feel terrible very soon."

"How do you know that? Levi was supposed to drug him." asked Rue

"I put MEK in his drink when I met him, well 'tripped' into him."

"What?"

"It's a solvent, it's in glue and paint etc. Pretty efficient actually."

He fell down on the floor from the chair he sat in and before Jasmin could ask Rue what they should do, Rue was already running towards him saying "I'm a doctor!"

His security started to gather around and secured the building. Two of his details came up to him and asked what they could do. "I'm fine." von Traufhsten said

"I think we should take him to a more private room so he can rest for a while." Rue said

"I'm fine, I just need to sit down for a second." he answered

"Only a couple of minutes then you'll be as good as new."
Rue tried to convince him

He looked around and saw how everybody was standing
looking at him and he agreed to go for a few minutes.
They helped him up and led him away, Jasmin started to
follow them. She said in the earpiece "Be ready in five."

"In stand-by."

Von Traufhsten laid down on a daybed in the viewing
room. Jasmin opened the door and they were far enough
away to use a gun. Rue gave the gun to Jasmin very
discreetly. Jasmin screwed on the silencer behind her
back and waited for the right moment.

One of his security details took out their phone after they
had whispered something to each other.

"Wouldn't do that." Jasmin said as she shot his
colleagues. He dropped his phone and reached for his
gun. She shot him in the head before he could make a
move. Von Traufhsten sat up and tried to scream for help.
Jasmin said to him "Sleep well!" and injected him with
more MEK.

They dragged him out of the room into a small hallway
with an emergency exit. "Be ready, I have no idea where
we are exciting." Rue said to the others

"Copy that."

"Levi, where are you? We are going." Jasmin said

"Go without me, I have been caught up in something." he answered

"This is why you never let him drive." Rue said to Jasmin

Jasmin and Rue each took an arm and put them on their shoulders. They opened the door and security was alerted.

"We are at the side with a newer building attached to it." Said Rue

"I think they are here then." Robin said to Pascal as he pointed on the map

The van drove up to them and they put him in the back and drove away. Jasmin tied von Traufhsten's hands behind his back and asked "Is there a safe house around here, they are going to notice any second he is gone."

"There is a garage here that is abandoned, no safe house though." said Pascal

"We will make it work." said Rue

Chapter Twenty One (Von Traufhsten)

They tied him to a hook in the middle of the garage and waited for him to wake up. Rue, who still had her earpiece in, asked "Levi, what are you doing? All I'm asking is for you to say something. Robin will trace you if you need help since you aren't saying anything."

Meanwhile he was in a high speed police chase that had gone on for about an hour.

"I'm fine, I don't need any help... at the moment. I have everything under control." Levi answered

Von Traufhsten started to wake up and Rue said

"Thank you for answering at least."

Once again she was going to ask nicely and then bring in Jasmin. Rue didn't like to do this stuff.

"Sleep well? I'll ask you one time and one time only. Who are you working with and what's your plan?" she asked

Von Traufhsten didn't answer, he just made some sounds and a while later he said "Don't understand."

"The question?" she asked

"Who are you?... The board, it's you!" he said with a heavy breath

"I'm feeling nice today so I'll give you one more try. Who are you working with and what's your plan?"

"I have no idea what you're talking about."

"Okay, well don't say I didn't give you a chance. He is all yours!"

"Hi, I'm a person who can help you out of this or make it worse and the choice is yours. If you just tell me the truth everything will be quick, but if you lie well honey I can't help you then." Jasmin said

He smiled at her and said "You're pathetic. People are missing me already, you fool."

"No I'm not the fool, she is." and pointed at Rue who was offended by what she just said. Jasmin continued "But the one you are working with, well let's just say she is not going to be happy that you are here and giving me all the information, is she?"

"She won't think that."

"But honey she already has." Jasmin said and turned around

"Why would I believe you? You have kidnapped me."

"I'm only a consequence because of your own actions."

Rue came up with a phone she took from one of his security and gave it to Jasmin so she could show von Traufhsten.

Concerning the security at the Citadel:
Do not follow Von Traufhsten. Stay with the valuables and protect them.
Kyle,
Security Central

"You see this was sent moments after you were taken. They don't care about you. Only themselves and her you work for of course. You are replaceable so is your security which you get from her. You really should have taken your own, they are at least loyal to you." Rue said

"No one is coming for you. So you are still sure you want to protect her when she does this to you?" Jasmin asked

Von Traufhsten looked defeated but still didn't say anything.

"Last chance before I start."

He still didn't say anything and Jasmin took out honey and poured it over him. She continued to take out a jar full of fire ants and dropped them on him.

His body started to itch but since he couldn't use anything to scratch it with it felt like he was on fire. He tried to hold it together for a couple of minutes, but was not able to. "Okay, fine! I have been dumping hazardous waste in a few rivers."

"Was that all?" Jasmin asked

"Mostly the sea."

Rue and Jasmin looked at each other with disgust but Rue seemed surprisingly happy about it. "This was one of the things that was probably true but we couldn't get concrete evidence and now I have a confession." Rue said

"Oh that is definitely a reason for the organization to want to get rid of him. Makes sense, makes sense." Jasmin said

Jasmin cleared her throat and said "Listen here you mass murderer, tell me what is your plan!"

"Why should I? I'm gonna die no matter what I say."

"A couple of reasons, get back at her for just abandoning you and I'll make it quick and painless. All this can be over."

"I'll make sure your wife is safe and taken care of if you tell us what you know" Rue reassured him

"I helped her fund her project and in return she would give me an easy way in with power. "

"We have already established that." Rue said annoyed

"She wanted revenge for her sibling and the guy who died knew what she was doing and some other person was also looking and following him... That's all I know I swear!"

"What is her next step?" Jasmin asked

"To find the only living evidence left, the person who followed the one that died."

"Remember any of their names?"

"I think they were high up in what you call um.. the organization. The other guy was here somewhere sometime. Trying to... She was one of two women in a man's world. That's what she always said. Please just get on with it, it still hurts like hell! I've held up my deal."

Jasmin took up the gun from the table and asked "Would you like to say something or pray?"

"Tell my wife I love her and please I'm begging you let someone find my body... so she can get some closure." he said holding back tears

"They will. I think everyone deserves to be found."
Jasmin nodded her head and pulled the trigger.

They were quiet for a few minutes before Jasmin asked
"The phone, how did you know?"

Rue laughed then smiled and said "Robin sent it from a
burner then changed the time I think. I don't really
know."

"Kyle?"

"Remember that guy we used to watch like he was in
videos or something? It was the first name that I thought
of." Rue said while she laughs

"Wait, so they are actually looking for him? We need to
get Pascal and Robin here and figure out where the hell
Levi is!"

Chapter Twenty Two (the last days of Waleed)

Pascal and Robin were back inside the garage and getting briefed by Jasmin while Rue cleaned her guns.

"Rue, call Kumar and see if he has any more information. Robin, you need to get working on Waleed's whereabouts the days before he died." Jasmin said

"Anybody, I need that help now." Levi said in the earpiece

"What have you done?" Rue answered

"Turn on the news, I can't explain now."

Rue told Robin to turn on a news channel and he did. It showed helicopter footage of a police chase. "Wait, is that Levi?" Robin asked surprised

"Of course, I let him drive and this happens again." Rue said disappointed

"Again!?" Robin said even more surprised than before

"Everybody get to work. Pascal, you fix this Levi problem, honestly." Jasmin said and threw an earpiece to him

Rue talked on the phone with Kumar who was stuck in traffic due to the police chase. "Yeah that's Levi." Rue said

"I have a copy of Aaron's phone records and he had contact with Waleed right before he died. Not only that but Aaron was supposed to be in Sweden not Waleed." Kumar said

"No wonder he went off the grid."

"Aaron hasn't left France yet, I think he is on foot trying to get out."

"Jasmin, get over here! Where would you leave the country if you were on foot?"

"Here, the terrain is good and an easy way out but that's just what I would do."

"We need to try to contact him. But we don't know where he gets his news from." Rue said

"I have an idea!" Jasmin said with a big smile on her face and called a number on her phone.

"Yes… Jasmin, I'm listening." the chairman answered with a big sigh

"We need to get in contact with Aaron Lane so he knows he is safe with us." Jasmin said

"Why?"

"He is going to be killed by Jade. Presumably."

"You sure it's Jade."

"Everything points to her sure as hell isn't Rue."

"What more do you need?" the chairman asked

"To pinpoint Aaron's exact location."

"I'll have a satellite track him." the chairman said before he hung up

Jasmin put down the phone and turned to and said "that was weird. He didn't say no."

"You really do have him wrapped around your finger." Kumar said who was still on the phone with Rue.

"If we get to Aaron I have done everything for nothing?" Robin asked

"No, it's still very valuable. Aaron can have missed something. Always good to be prepared." Jasmin reassured him

"And now you can focus on helping Pascal fix the Levi situation." Rue contributed

Chapter Twenty Three (the Levi situation)

Robin put in an earpiece and traced Pascal and Levi to see their locations. He also put the tab with the news on his second monitor.

"Pascal, Levi, what's your situation?" Robin asked

"I'm running low on fuel and I don't really know where I am." Levi said confused

"I'm on my way from the garage but I'm stuck. Can you get the traffic to start moving?" asked Pascal

"I'll do my best." Robin said

He started to change the traffic lights to clear the path for Pascal and at the same time block the police. He looked at the map despret trying to find an alternative route for Levi.

"Levi, turn left."

"What!? It's a construction site!" Levi yelled

"Do it, then right then left then jump."

"Jump?!"

"With the car!" Robin exclaimed

"That's even too much for me. You are trying to kill me, aren't you?"

"I'm not like you. Just trust me for once in your life."

"Yeah in my short life." Levi said

He was speeding through the construction site to the end of the road. He closed his eyes and prepared for the worst. The car left the ground for a second and he started to scream and then it landed. He had his foot on the brake and was standing still.

"Levi! Go, go, go! What are you waiting for?" Robin screamed

Levi opened his eyes and looked around then started to realize what had happened.

"Levi! What are you doing? Go!" Robin continued

He started to hear the sirens and snapped out of it and drove away.

"Now what?" he asked

"Pascal will meet you soon, hang tight. Pascal you drive to the right on the sidewalk in twenty meters then drive into the park in the direction of the playground." Robin explained

Pascal did what Robin said and tried not to hit any people who were standing still in complete shock. The police now had Pascal on their radar and Robin said "Jasmin I need your help. Pascal, go to the left. It should be an ally there and be on standby. Levi you keep driving forward till I say otherwise."

"Yes." Jasmin said

"We need a distraction for the police just for one minute. Can you fix that."

"On it." she said

"I can't drive forward anymore left or right?" Levi asked

"Forward, go forward!"

"I can't!"

"Keep going forward! Stay inside the car no matter what." Robin said

Robin kept on multitasking and tried to get an escape route in place for them. Jasmin gave Robin a thumbs up from the otherside of the garage.

"Robin the road is almost over!" Levi said frighted

"Pascal, go to the coordinates I'm sending you."

"Will do!"

"Levi listen to me very carefully, roll down your window then wait till the car is almost full of water then swim forward towards the direction you are going now."

Levi took off his seatbelt and started to swim up towards the surface. When he got up he asked Robin "What do I do now?"

"Run as fast as you can till the bushes and wait for the police to turn off the lights and sirens."

"Jasmin now!" Robin said

She called a number she got from the chairman and said "Requesting all units to stand down. I repeat, stand down."

Then an associate to the organization would impersonate the dispatcher to then say this to all of the units in pursuit of Levi.

"Levi, run out onto the road right now as fast as you can. Pascal be ready to pick him up and keep driving in that direction and take the third exit." Robin said

Levi, who was soaking wet, ran out to the van and got in. Pascal drove away when they heard the sirens again.

"Now what?" Pascal asked

"Drive and change cars then come back before the sun is up."

Jasmin hugged Robin and said "That was awesome!"

Chapter Twenty Four (Cléron)

It was a late morning when Jasmin got a text from the chairman:

Aaron's latest position: 47.083004, 6.087105
South East Cléron

"Wake up, time to go. Wait, where is Kumar?"

Robin, who was already awake said "He is out with Pascal jogging I think."

"Levi, Rue, Chop chop!"

"You're not even dressed yet." Levi said tired

"Up!" Jasmin said

Jasmin started to get ready and was deciding which dress she would wear when Kumar and Pascal got into the garage.

"Pascal, get the car ready. We are going to Cléron. Pretty accurate where Jasmin said she would actually go." Rue said and threw a package of wet wipes to him.

"Thank you" said Pascal and handed over it to Kumar.

"You're a genius. You know that right." Kumar said

"They are always in my go bags. Highly recommend it." Jasmin said

They got in the car and started to drive towards the coordinates on the map.

"This looks unreal, never seen anything like this." said Rue in awe

"True!" Jasmin said in agreement

Pascal parked the car and said "Can't drive any further. Where do you want me?"

Jasmin answered "In standby and lookout."

Rue, Levi, Robin, Kumar and Jasmin walked into the woods.

"Oh shit, the chairman never told me whether or not he had made contact with Aaron."

"That's not good." Rue said quietly

"Why not?" Robin asked

"Are you stupid or something? He doesn't know he is safe with us if that is the case." Levi said annoyed

"Language." Rue said

"I forgot about that, wait, wait, wait he is going to kill us." Robin said frightened

"Kumar, you talk then. You knew Waleed better then any of us." said Levi

"I never pictured this was how I was going to die. Friendly fire by one of the board members in a wood in France. This is why I'm behind a screen."

"Robin, shut up! He is not gonna kill us."

"A world class assassin on the run from the world's biggest organization, feeling threatened. Yeah no definitely not." said Robin sarcastically

Chapter Twenty Five (Aaron Lane)

Jasmin who had been ahead of the rest of the group said "Kumar, something to make Aaron trust us."

"I'm thinking!"

"Think faster, we are closing in."

Kumar tried to think of something only the three of them would know. He finally remembered something and shouted the loudest he could, "Twenty eight burgers!"

Everyone looked confused at Kumar while he continued to shout.

"You scared him away with whatever that was." Levi said

Meanwhile up in a tree a man was looking at them through the scope of his rifle.

"He can't be far away, the ashes are still warm." Jasmin confirmed and took a look around.

"Twenty eight burgers!" Kumar keep on shouting

They all looked at each other to make sense of what Kumar was saying.

"Why... What?"

"I have no clue."

"Hands up! Make yourselves known." a voice said

They all turned around trying to find where the sound came from and Kumar said "Aaron? We need your help. Rue, Jasmin, Levi, Robin and me Kumar are here. Twenty eight burgers. Waleed trusted me with information after his death."

The man jumped down from the tree.

"Twenty eight burgers, huh." Aaron said while he laught

"It worked?"

"One of the papers from the box I sent, right?"

"Can't believe that actually worked." Levi said

Chapter Twenty Six (the evidence)

Aaron took out a USB drive from his jack pocket and said "I believe this is what you are looking for."

"Jasmin four cars incoming. What do you want me to do?" Pascal said in the earpiece

"Drive away now! Pick us up when it's safe."

"We need to run." Jasmin said to the others

"Here!" Aaron said and threw the thumb drive to Rue

She looked confused and he continued while climbing up the tree. "They probably don't know you are here. I take care of myself, you make sure the evidence gets to the board."

"He is right." Jasmin said

"Thank you!" Levi said and smiled at him

They started to run through the woods as fast as they could and Jasmin took the lead.

"You know... they will kill him." Robin said gasping for air

Aaron sat waiting and tried to control his breathing. He knew he couldn't let them go after the others but he tried to keep them long enough to give them a head start.

The men who presumably worked for Jade went to the fireplace and one said "Not cold, he is here somewhere."

The men started to walk away when Aaron had to make a move to get them to stay in this area. He broke off a branch and threw it to the ground. The men pointed their weapons in all directions trying to find Aaron. One of them said "It was probably just an animal."

Then Aaron shot one in the back of his head and they started to shoot against the tree.

Back at the group who had now stopped running and were walking to let Robin catch his breath.

Rue put her earpiece in and asked "Pascal, where are you?"

"Just keep that direction, I'll find a way for you."

"I can send my location to you."

"Already have it. Spent to much time with Robin." he said jokingly

They heard a gunshot in the distance followed by many more and they started to run again.

"I can't... need.. stop!" Robin tried his best to say

They didn't answer him and continued to run.

"Pascal, update." Jasmin said

"Get to the road."

"There is no bloody road." Rue said irritated

"You are beside it!"

"No..." Rue only had time to say before Jasmin saw the road "Here!"

Everybody was standing on the small road and waited for Pascal to show up. They saw a small yellow car driving like a maniac and Levi said "You gotta be kidding me." Pascal drove up to them and said "Get in!"

Jasmin got in the passenger seat and Kumar took the seat behind. Leaving Rue, Levi and Robin only with one real seat.

"Rue in." Levi said

"So you can get the only good seat?"

"Seriously!" Jasmin said

Rue got in then Levi and Robin had to sit on the floor with Jasmin's legs.

"What the hell is this?! Why did you take this clown for a getaway car?" Levi said squished in the back

"It was the only one who would fit on these roads." Pascal said defencive

"Well, we don't fit."

"Rue, do you have the drive?" Jasmin asked calmly

Rue panicked for a second before she found it in her jack pocket and said "Yes!"

"Wait, all of our stuff?" Jasmin said worryingly

"In the back."

Jasmin patted him on the shoulder and said "Thank you!"

Chapter Twenty Seven (the getaway)

They had driven for about fifteen minutes when Jasmin's phone buzzed. She looked at it and said "It's the chairman. He wants us to know we are being followed and they have blocked all the road ahead."

"Guess we are going off road then." Pascal said and drove right onto a field.

He drove on small dirt roads with holes in it and Robin repeatedly hit his head on the glove compartment. Rue is slamming into both Levi and Kumar.

"Please get on the road." Robin begged

"Stop complaining." Pascal said

"Oh that's rich coming from you Mr. I have my own seat." Levi said from the backseat

They continued to argue and then Jasmin said "Can we not do this right now? Focus on how we can get away from... You could have avoided that! You are doing it on purpose!"

Pascal hit a large root making Jasmin hit her head against the roof. They looked shocked at her since she usually was the calm one.

"Road, road, road, road!" Rue shrieked in excitement

Pascal made a hefty turn and they were on an asphalt road.

"Which way!"

"Right no, the other right." Rue said from the backseat

"Where are we even going?" Kumar asked

"Away!" Jasmin said as her phone once again buzzed.

"If we weren't being chased this would be beautiful. We are in Flagey. So cool." Rue said

"The chairman says:
Airfield Pontarlier, propeller plane ready for pilot on arrival
Best regards,
The chairman" Jasmin read loud to the others

"Should we leave the country? Robin asked

"Depending on where Jade is, I think I might just know exactly how to find out." Jasmin said with a big smile on her face

They drove into Pontarlier and abandoned the car in a parking lot to blend in with the other. Pascal got the plane ready for take off and the other was talking about how to get Jade out of hiding.

"You see all this is because of her brother Lyle, revenge and his wife never went back to being the French ambassador in the states after Lyle died. She is going to assume her new role as the french minister plenipotentiary in Finland next week. I believe that if Sylvie needed help Jade would come." Jasmin explained

"What would be believable for her to ask about?" asked Rue

"I'll see what I can find. By the way, the drive is encrypted. Can't see what's on it right now." Robin said and started typing on his computer

"I have a question, couldn't the chairman say he needed a meeting or something with her? " Levi said

"Maybe she will be a no show?"

Jasmin took out her phone and called the chairman.

He sighed and said "Jasmin."

"What is better? You set up a meeting and Jade will come or she will come to her brother's wife's help."

"Both." he said and hung up the phone

"What did he say?" Kumar asked her

"Both." Jasmin said confused

"Oh hello, she... his wife has a property that she inherited after him. It's outside Paris in Melun." said Robin

Chapter Twenty Eight (Melun)

They had been flying for a while when Pascal said "We will land soon."

Pascal had found them a car and they were driving through Melun to the safehouse.

"It is so beautiful, I'm shocked. France really is the most beautiful rare gem." Rue said once again

"It truly is." Kumar agreed

Jasmin sat and read Jade's file time after time to find any liabilities but the only one was her brother who is dead.

"Tell me everything about Jade and I mean everything you know. What she eats, her childhood, everything." she said to the others

"They were raised by their uncle and he died many years back. Jade has no other known family members alive except his wife Sylvie. She likes steak." Rue said

"She blamed the organization for his death then suddenly didn't." Levi said

"Okay so she has no family except Lyle's wife. Does she have access to where they grew up or her brother's house or something? Once again not in this file the chairman gave me. I don't get what he is hiding but it sure is something."

"I read an article about them before and looked at their estates. Her uncle sold his house before he passed. Just a second, ah here.

The Toussaints spend their day off by talking to their families back in France. When we asked Ambassador Toussaints if she regretted taking on this responsibility she answered as you would expect. "Never, I'm very fond of my work as Ambassador. I'm very honored to be trusted with my country like this."

Her husband on the other hand said that he misses his late fathers hunting cabin. "We visit as often as we can. We have our families nearby and actually sold our apartment in Paris as we didn't use it anymore."

They reassured the French citizens that the Ambassador always has the best interest of her country. "Don't be afraid to come up to us if you see us. We love to talk with the people we represent."

"Robin, great work today! Still no word from the chairman I called, he didn't answer. So should we just go in the morning if we haven't heard from him?"

"I could use a shower and a bed." Levi said

"Yeah, I want to look around in the most beautiful place on earth." Rue agreed

"If he has some other plan, we could ruin that if we do it on our own." said Kumar to Jasmin

"Since when... what?" she looked confused and continued "I was the one who said it first, stop trying to convince me."

They all looked at her and breathed out in relief. They went into the house and saw that it only had one bed and no electricity. Robin desperately tried every light switch and started to whine. He goes over to the bed and says "At least we have a bed." and sits on it.

He lay down when the legs on the side he sat on gave out and he fell to the floor and said "I'm actually gonna cry!"

The other ones who were used to this tried not to laugh at him as he dragged the mattress away from the broken bed.

"Robin, hey we got a roof over our heads." Levi said to annoy him and Rue hit his arm.

"Not for long, if he says it." Pascal joked with Levi

Robin, Kumar and Rue slept on the mattress while Pascal had gone out to the car. Levi and Jasmin had a blanket on the floor but when Levi woke up Kumar had gone to him and Jasmin was on the mattress. He looked confused around and he turned around to try to get some more sleep. Then Jasmin's phone started to ring.

She answered "Hi, what's up?"

"I have had surveillance on Mrs. Toussaint and Jade. Jade is not in the house or surrounding areas. I have sent out during the night a summon to a meeting. How do you plan to execute this?" said the chairman

"Lure her out posing as Sylvie and then she is officially on your radar?" she said with an unsure voice

"All the organization's resources and associates are on standby, whatever you need to make Jade believe you. I don't care what you do or how you do it, make her believe."

"Yes, Sir." Jasmin answer and he hung up

"Did Jasmin unironically just say Sir?" Rue asked

"Who?" Kumar and Levi said at the same time

"He said I could do whatever, however I want to and he had summoned you to a meeting." Jasmin explained

"Oh yeah, I see that now." Levi said as he checked his phone.

"More details to come, emergency meeting." Kumar read from his phone

Chapter Twenty Nine (the plans)

"He has never given someone permission to do this before." Rue said

"Yeah, we should have voted on it and seen what the consequences could be." said Kumar

"The whole point is to not let Jade know, can't vote on it if she is there." Levi said

"I know that was just stating a fact."

"What if we got Robin arrested?" Levi suggested

"What?!" Robin said in shock

"Wait, no that is actually smart Levi." said Jasmin

"Excuse me? What?" Robin continued

"She wanted to frame you, so why not do that?" Rue said

"You know what that is perfect. I'm going to arrange that right now." Jasmin said and took out her phone

"I don't want that." Robin said offended

"Not you 'you' the police in Sweden will go to 'your' house and it will be something big, so it's on the news and then Jade will believe that she is somewhat safe. If I understood it correctly." Kumar explained

"Then we get her brother's wife to lure her out. So she is on the radar." said Levi

"Holy hell, you are on a roll today." Rue said in awe

Levi continued "Maybe we can make her believe Aaron is outside her house?"

"No, she would know if Aaron was killed or not and we don't at the moment. It's too big of a risk." Rue said

"Von Traufhsten no one knows if he is alive or not except us, he could have escaped. She wouldn't know that." Jasmin contributed

They continued to discuss the plan and how to execute it.

Jasmin interrupted the others and read from an article published seconds ago.

The Swedish National Task Force is handling a delicate situation due to the suspect being considered extremely dangerous and all authorities are on high alert.

The authorities were not willing to give out anymore information due to the sensitive nature of the situation.

"How will she believe that is Robin? It can be literally anyone." said Kumar

"But 'Robin' is going to walk out of that house on live TV. Just wait and see and when you put the chairman's message it becomes obvious don't you think?"

"So 'von Traufhsten' will do the same to Jade's brother's wife. Ah I get it now." Robin said overly proud over himself

"Let's get to work and where the hell is Pascal, someone update him." Rue said

Chapter Thirty (the Toussaints)

Robin got a notification on his phone and read out loud:

"New information released about the shocking news in Sweden. The suspect is a man in his late 30's and his wife was earlier today brought in for questioning.

A reliable source said "This is related with the murder in the car bomb earlier this month."

"I know it's very easy to manipulate the truth, never witnessed it live like this though." Rue said

"But you're Norwegian right? Sweden, what?"

"I live there with my wife, her family is from there and I get to keep working with Jasmin. Win-Win" Robin explained

The chairman sent a message again:

"East Ruston, Norwich, England 12.00 local time, thursday
Outside the reaches
The leak has been taken care of. New board member needs to be selected due to the extended time being up."

"Okay let's do this!" Jasmin said and put a bag in the car

One associate to the organization who looked like Von Traufhsten got in the car and Jasmin began getting him ready.

She ruffled up his hair and put dirt in it, to make it seem like he had been out in the woods for a while. She used some fake blood and gave him makeup to look like he had been tortured and was dehydrated.

"Remember what the plan is?" Jasmin asked him just to be sure

"Yes ma'am!"

She gave him Von Traufhsten's actual clothes from the night he died and put a microphone in a pocket and said "Ready to go!"

He got out of the car and into the woods up towards Sylvie's cabin. When he got close, he got into character.

He crawled up the stairs and banged on the door and when she opened the only thing he said was "Jade."

He laid on the kitchen floor and didn't let her help him while continued to only say "Jade."

She picked up the phone and called a number.

"Yes, Hi I would like to speak with Jade." and after a while of back and forth finally she got through to Jade.

Kumar, who understood French, translated everything they could hear.

"Sylvie is saying that a man is in her kitchen asking for her and now she describes him."

Sylvie put the phone on speaker and let the impersonator talk with Jade. She asks him in English what happened but he only continued to say Jade before passing out.

"Now Sylvie is saying he looks to be in really bad shape. Something and Sylvie... oh she is getting mad."

"What?" everyone else said to him

"Right of course I'm sorry she was saying how this was Jade's problem and she didn't have time for all this and now I think Jade agreed to come and pick him up or she ordered a sandwich. Can't tell." Kumar constituted

"Pretty obvious which one it is." Rue said irritated

Robin had already begun to track the call and was trying to find a possible location.

"It only pinged on one tower can't give you anymore now." he said

A black sedan drove up to them and two men in black suits came up to the driver seat.

"Are you Mr. Rose-Mary on the second?" One of them asked

"Yes." Pascal asked and unlocked the doors for them.

They opened the back door and Jasmin gave them each an earpiece and said "On my word go and pick him up and then ask the woman for the phone she contacted Jade with and send a text saying you will drive him to rest up."

"Got it!" both said at the same time

Then they sat quiet for a little while when Levi said "Hey Robin, I'm sorry."

"I just encrypted the evidence and wow." Robin answered

Before anyone had the chance to ask anything he said "Just got her on the organization's radar."

"Guys, go now!" Jasmin said to the men in the sedan

The car drove away and the men got out and knocked on the door.

"Can I help you?" Sylvie asked

"You have a man here ,Von Traufhsten and we will get him checked out before he meets Jade."

Sylvie didn't hesitate and let them inside to carry him away into the backseat of the car.

"One more thing ma'am could I just take a quick peek on the phone you called Jade from."

"Why?" she asked suspiciously

"Just to ensure the safety and privacy of Mr. Von Traufhsten. Ms. Jade said so herself and gave clear instructions. It won't take long."

Jasmin told him what to say
"He loved his cabin more than me. Jade trusts us with her own life."

Sylvie handed over the phone and the man sent a text saying: *We have picked up the delivery and will check him out and you will get the package when it's secure.*

He quickly deleted the message as soon as it was sent and handed back the phone then said "Have a lovely day Mrs. Toussaint!"

Chapter Thirty One (on the radar)

"Guess we are headed towards the meeting now?" Pascal asked

"Yeah." said Rue

"We need a few planes going to East Ruston from all around if she would look for anything. Just to be sure." Jasmin said on the phone to the chairman

"It's.... already in process. Is it done?" he asked

"Yes, she's out."

"You are expected at the meeting with the evidence."

"Yeah, no shit." Jasmin said and hung up

The others stared at her when Levi said "What is wrong with you?"

"She has a problem with authorities." Robin answered as Pascal drove away.

They drove from Sylvie's cabin for about 35 minutes to a small airfield.

They got out of the car and and on to a midsize jet.

"Finally get to rest." Robin said as he laid down.

"Pascal, time?" Jasmin asked

"I would say roughly four hours."

"Thanks." she said and sat down besides Rue

They landed a few towns over and Levi, Rue and Kumar disembarked the plane and waited for a car to come and pick them up. Pascal also went outside to check on the plane and waited outside till the car approted.

He started to get everything ready for take off again and said "You can come up, but stay low."

Out of the cargo compartment, Jasmin crawled out and sat down on the floor.

"Robin?" she said confused

"I'm stuck!" he answered while struggling out of the opening.

Jasmin gripped his arms and heaved Robin up.

Pascal turned around and shortly after they were up in the air again. But only for a short while and once again he landed the plane.

"I drive." said Jasmin and took the keys to the van out of Pascal's hand.

Meanwhile Rue, Levi and Kumar were almost at the meeting place.

"I don't know why I'm so nervous." said Kumar

"Well if it goes wrong, it's only the end of the world as we know it and our life. Yeah."

"Thanks, Rue. " Kumar said sarcastically

"I wish Jasmin were here so she could call the chairman." Levi said

Chapter Thirty Two (the arrival)

They were outside the reaches and tried to find their entrance.

"There!" said Rue and pointed at a door with a flower crown of daffodils and gladiolus hanging from it.

"He is literally obsessed over flowers that are called lilies." said Levi as he opened the door

A few of the members were already there.

"Have any of you heard from Aaron?" Ninos asked

Rue hesitated before she said "No we haven't."

"Hope he shows up today." said Conrad

"Where are the others?" Kumar asked

"So we are missing Kwame, the chairman, Aaron, Jade and Christian. Well Waleed also may he rest in peace." said Ray

It was ten minutes before the meeting was supposed to start. The door opened and Kwame walked in with his cane and behind him was the chairman.

"I've... spoken to Jade and Christian today. No word from Aaron Lane. We may have to... activate Order nr. 23." the chairman said to the other members

They had sat in silence for a couple of minutes and then the door opened and Jade walked in and Christian closed the door behind them.

"We have gathered here today... for the leak has been dealt with. It was our candidate for Waleed's place, Robin. He is now in our hands. The time for Waleed's replacement is up. We will all say a nominee." the chairman said

Jasmin drove up the van to the front of the house beside the one the members were in. They turned on their earpieces and realized that neither Levi, Kumar or Rue had theirs on.

"Shit, this is not very great. Time to improvise then I guess." Jasmin said

"No, no, no stick to the plan." Robin said

"How? I have literally no idea what they are doing or which room they are in." Jasmin said irritated

Robin was biting his nail and said "You know what? Fuck the plan!"

Jasmin and Pascal looked confused at each other.

He continued, "Go in, I'll guide you."

Jasmin took the drive and went out of the car. Pascal turned around and stared at Robin.

"I'm getting very good now aren't I?" Robin said as he took out the thermal camera out of its bag.

"Anyone!" Jasmin said frustrated

"They should be in the living room. There are apparently two people upstairs from what I can see." he said while looking at the schematics and the camera.

"Hope to the goddesses that they are in the right positions."

Flashback to when they were in the plane:
Rue, Levi, Jasmin, Kumar and Robin were talking about the plan.

"You have to sit with your backs against the window or windows, whatever. Find a wall where a bullet won't ricochet and where she can't easily escape with an alternative route." Jasmin explained

Present time:
Jasmin walked through the door and locked it behind her. She was wearing a magic green evening dress with silver details. She walked down a few steps and into the living room where everyone sat in complete silence and looked at her. Jade sat at a relatively good place or at least she could work with it.

"Hi! I'm Jasmin. You probably have heard and talked about me. Mr. Chairman was so generous and invited me here to have a presentation for all of you. Shall we begin?"

Everyone looked confused at each other. But didn't say anything since it's not their place to question the chairman.

While Jasmin got everything ready Jade became noticeably stressed and anxious. To invite someone to a meeting had never happened before but neither have one of their own betrayed them this way. Jade slowly moved her chair and said "Can I go and get some water?"

"It's water on the table." said Ray who sat besides her

"I want it fresh."

The chairman gave her a nod and she walked the way towards the kitchen but quickly changed her direction to the door instead. She pulled the door handle but Jasmin had locked it and she felt an excruciating pain. Jasmin had tased her and Kumar and Levi came over so they could restrain her. The other members were frightened but the chairman quickly said "Everything will be explained. Don't worry."

Jasmin said "You can come in now."

Chapter Thirty Three (the conclusion)

The door opened and Robin came in. Rue got up to help the others carry Jade back to her seat.

"Okay what... is this?" Ray asked shocked

"Long story short Jade was the leak." said Jasmin

"Long story?" asked Conrad

"We'll tell everything... Show all the evidence. Then we vote." said the chairman

They gave Jade some sedative and began to explain.

"The question is what should we do with her? Integration and then end it? Or the hole? Suggestions are welcomed." said the chairman

Kumar, Rue and Levi took their places at the table. The other members stared at the chairman like something was supposed to happen.

"Robin is not a member yet... But Article Nr. 85 states." he said and took out a large book from a briefcase on the floor. It was a black leather cover with gold writing:

Book of Orders (1930)

Para bellum,
In omnia paratus,
Exitus acta probat

"In an abnormal or uncertain event, where a decision needs to be made expeditious, the Chairman has the authority to appoint one or more acting board members. The decision has to be evaluated in due course." the chairman read from the book

"You have your chauffeur with you?" he asked Jasmin

"In the car."

"Bring him to me."

Jasmin unmuted the earpiece and asked Pascal to go inside. The chairman called out for someone upstairs. As Pascal got in, a young woman came down the stairs and said "Yes."

"Sit, you are now a temporary member... and I expect you to be etiquette. This is my granddaughter Eugenia Myers. She is exceptional... tell them." the chairman continued

She awkwardly held up her hand and said hi to the board members who sat at the table.

"Go ahead."

"I study law at Yale. You can call me Ninni or Nia." she said before the chairman stopped her and said "You call her Miss Eugenia Myrers and nothing else... Am I clear?"

"Jasmin Burton, Robin Elden, the chauffeur ..." he waited for someone to fill him in. Robin whispered "Pascal Edwards" "Yes, Pascal Edwards, Eugenia Myers are now... in the time being acting board members."

"Sir, since Jade is not a participant, will this go through the order as a regular meeting?" Conrad asked

"Conrad Haas you'll be acting as Primary Minute Taker, since you are secondary and Levi will be Secondary... as the arrangement states." the chairman said

"I've already started since Jasmin came into the room. But here you can start with the announcement of acting board members." Conrad said quietly to Levi and handed over his notes

Jasmin started from the beginning, at the charity gala in Sweden where she first saw Waleed. She continued until everyone had gotten the information, which took about an hour. The chairman then said to Jasmin that she could take her seat.

He cleared his throat and said "The alternatives are 'Kill Jade right here right now' or 'put in the hole/interrogate then execute' Since there are members who are unfamiliar with the voting, Ninos can you explain?"

"Put up one finger like this and wait for Mr. Chairman's word." she explained

"Kill Jade Toussaint at the present moment. All in favor!" The chairman waited a few more seconds, but nobody put up their hand or said anything. He countinted "Interrogation method: being put in the hole, then executed. All in favor!"

Everyone held up their hand and the experienced members all said "Aye." Conrad nodded at the chairman who then said "A unanimous vote, that is excellent news due to it regarding a member of the organization. The decision is 'Interrogation method: being put in the hole' does anyone oppose? Speak now or be forever silent." The chairman waited ten seconds and then hit his knuckles against the table.

"Meetings over!"

"What now?" asked Robin

"Go on about your day." Levi answered

Everyone started to get up and called or texted their chauffeur's when the chairman said "Ray, Cruz and Levi you follow with us to make sure Jade gets to the destination without any unforeseen events."

"Yes, sir!" the three said simultaneously. They carried her to the chairman's car and Levi hugged goodbye to Rue, Jasmin and Kumar. When he got to Robin he said "Hey man, I know we had our differences but this wouldn't have been possible without you."

Robin forced a smile and shook his hand.

The man upstairs came down with Eugenia's bag and he and Ninos waited for her in the car. "Grandpa! See you at home." she said and got in the car. Kwame and Conrad then left together.

"Kumar, which airport?" Rue asked

"LHR. Heathrow"

"That works, we can share a car then."

The chairman's car drove away with Ray following the car. Rue hugged Jasmin, Robin and Pascal and she got in the car where Kumar already was and he said goodbye through the window.

"Jasmin, Robin where are you headed?" Pascal asked

"Home, a lot of series to catch up on." she laughed

 "Home to my pregnant wife."

"What?! She is pregnant. Why didn't you say something? Congratulations!" she said as she hugged him

"Alright, home it is then." Pascal said with a smile on his face and then they got in the car and were about to leave the driveway when a car came speeding back to the house. Jasmin got out of the car when she saw it was Kumar and Rue's car.

"What's wrong?" Jasmin asked

Rue didn't answer and kept going towards Jasmin. She gently pushed Jasmin's hair from her face and kissed her.

"It won't be like last time I promise. When I'm with you I'm so much happier. No one understands me except you. I won't disappear again, I'm ready to face it." Rue said

Jasmin smiled and opened the car door for Rue and she got in and Robin said "Finally! Pascal you owe me 20."

Kumar's car drove slowly away and Pascal drove out right behind them on the small road.